Ann Schweninger

Birthday Wishes

Viking Kestrel

For Geoffrey Hayes

VIKING KESTREL
Viking Penguin Inc., 40 West 23rd Street, New York, New York 10010, U.S.A.
Penguin Books Ltd, Harmondsworth, Middlesex, England
Penguin Books Australia Ltd, Ringwood, Victoria, Australia
Penguin Books Canada Limited, 2801 John Street, Markham, Ontario, Canada L3R 1B4
Penguin Books (N.Z.) Ltd, 182–190 Wairau Road, Auckland 10, New Zealand

Copyright © Ann Schweninger, 1986
All rights reserved

First published in 1986 by Viking Penguin Inc.
Published simultaneously in Canada

Printed in Japan by Dai Nippon.
1   2   3   4   5   90   89   88   87   86

Library of Congress Cataloging in Publication Data
Schweninger, Ann.   Birthday wishes.
Summary: The Rabbit family's festivities for Buttercup's
fifth birthday make all her wishes come true.
[1. Rabbits—Fiction.   2. Birthdays—Fiction.   3. Parties—Fiction]   I. Title.
PZ7.S41263Bi   1986   [E]   85-20178   ISBN 0-670-80742-7

Getting Ready

Presents

Birthday List

roller skates
paints
dresses
bicycle
bubble gum
piano
tea set
doll
umbrella
sandals
puzzle
make-up set
puppet
yoyo
bracelet
toy bear
kite

Buttercup's Birthday

Party!

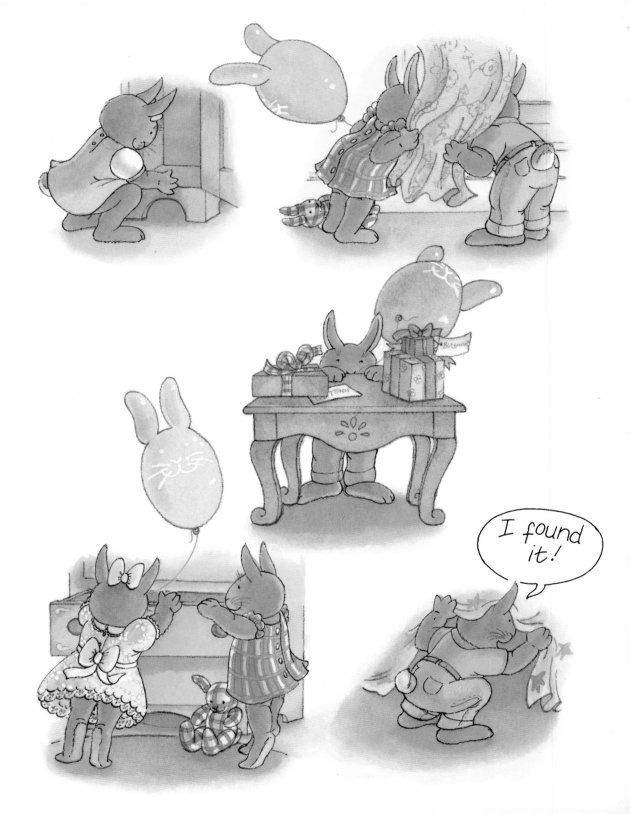

Opening Presents